Table of Contents

Rourke™

Can you find these words?

angry

chance

mistakes

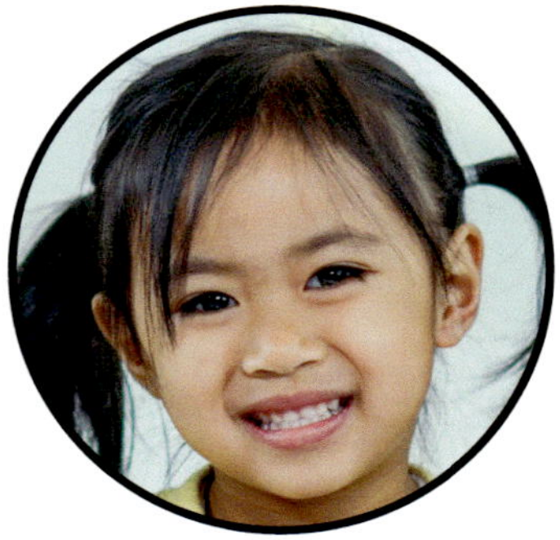

think

Getting Along

Getting along means being friendly and kind.

How do we get along?

We **think** about how others feel.

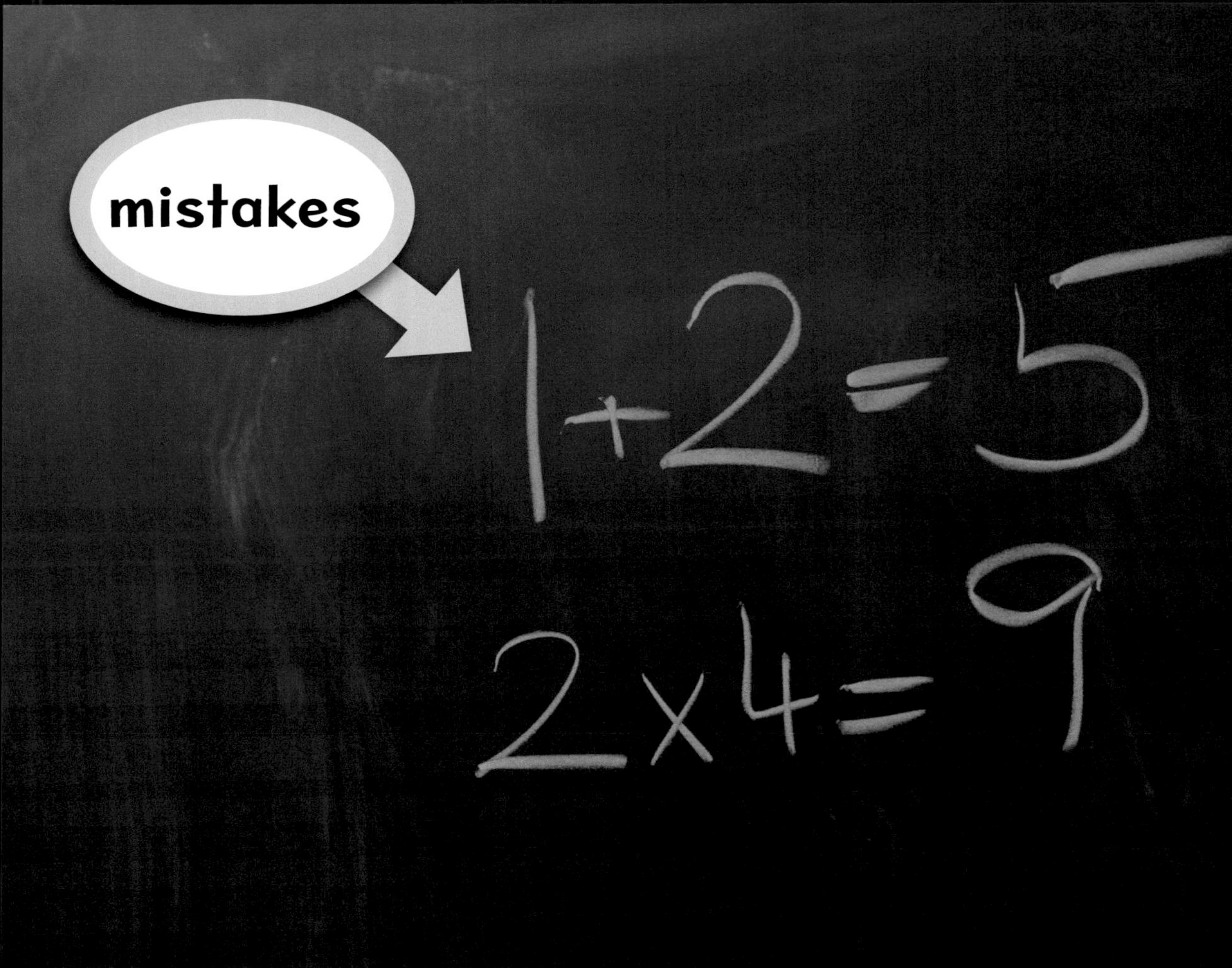

We don't laugh at our friends' **mistakes**.

We do not hit if we are **angry**.

We use words to share our feelings.

We take turns when we play.

We give everyone a **chance**.

We listen to others.
We show that we care.

Did you find these words?

We do not hit if we are **angry**.

We give everyone a **chance**.

We don't laugh at our friends' **mistakes**.

We **think** about how others feel.

Photo Glossary

angry (ANG-gree): Being mad or showing upset feelings toward someone.

chance (chans): The opportunity to do something.

mistakes (mis-STAKES): Things done incorrectly or wrong.

think (thingk): To use your mind to form an idea or solve a problem.

Index

About the Author

Terri Fields likes reading with and writing for children. When she's not reading or writing, she likes walking on the beach.

www.rourkebooks.com

PHOTO CREDITS: Cover ©JohnnyGreig, Page 2, 10-11,14,15 ©fstop123, Page 2,4-5,14,15 ©FatCamera, Page 2,6-7,14,15 ©Mattomedia Werbeagentur, Page 2,8-9,14,15 ©baona, Page 3 ©Rawpixel, Page 9-10 ©ImagineGolf, Page 12 ©Lordn

Edited by: Keli Sipperley
Cover design by: Kathy Walsh
Interior design by: Rhea Magara-Wallace

Library of Congress PCN Data
Getting Along / Terri Fields
(I Wonder)
ISBN (hard cover)(alk. paper) 978-1-64156-185-3
ISBN (soft cover) 978-1-64156-241-6
ISBN (e-Book) 978-1-64156-292-8
Library of Congress Control Number: 2017957794

Rourke Educational Media
Printed in the United States of America
01-3182211937